Tooter Scooter

Alicia P Zubot

Tooter Scooter
Copyright © 2020 by Alicia P Zubot

Tellwell Talent
www.tellwell.ca

ISBN
978-0-2288-2796-2 (Hardcover)
978-0-2288-2795-5 (Paperback)

To all children (and children at heart) in hospitals around the world,
or who are receiving care for a medical condition.
Have hope, take courage, and never give up!

Scooter the kitty lived in a galaxy far, far away on a planet called Zubot (*zoo-bot*). Only cats and kittens lived on this wee little planet.

Scooter was a different kind of kitten, because he had a bit of a problem.

He tooted a lot ... and I mean A LOT! He tooted when walking, when eating, and when playing. He even tooted when taking his long-needed naps!

One day after Scooter had finished eating a nice yummy breakfast, he decided to go outside to play with his kitten friends. As he was running, leaping, and sneaking (kittens like to sneak), he felt a big balloon of air fill up his belly.

Uh oh! he said to himself.
"Here we go again!" All of a sudden,
KAPOWWW!
KAPLEWEEE!!!

Scooter shot up into the air higher and higher ... and HIGHER! He left the atmosphere of Planet Zubot and zoomed like a rocket all the way to Planet Earth—a very long way!

Scooter landed on a choo-choo-train. It was filled with many weird-looking creatures that he had never seen before. Just as he relaxed back into a seat, he let out a
TOOOOOOT!

Poor Scooter, he didn't mean to toot!

All of the creatures screamed and shouted and quickly ran to the back of the train out of the way.

The train came to a stop, and Scooter hopped off. He had arrived at the Great Wall of China.

"What a majestic sight," Scooter said to himself, and he began to walk its curious, long path. Scooter came across some interesting-looking black and white creatures. They were really big compared to wee little Scooter. Just as he was about to ask these furry things for directions to his home planet, Scooter went

KAPOWWW!

His toot scared the panda bears, and they all ran away.

Poor little Scooter, he didn't mean to toot!

Scooter kept walking. He walked and walked until he came to an airport. He boarded an airplane and went so high that he could see all of the pretty trees, lakes, and hills below. Just as Scooter was about to take a photograph, he let out a
TOOOOOOT!
The airplane went loop-de-loop, all twisty-turny and this way and that. The airplane pilot quickly landed safely on the ground.

Poor Scooter, he didn't mean to toot!

When Scooter hopped off the airplane, he gasped in sure glee.

What a sight to see! he thought to himself.

Scooter's eyes became wide as he saw a circus show. The circus director said in a booming voice, "Come join in the fun, little kitty. We need a new act, and you're just the right cat!"

Scooter learned how to leap, twirl, and swing on the flying trapeze. His big moment came on that very same day, when he could show Planet Earth that he was super-cute, fluffy fun! Just as he made his last swing ... HURRAY ... Scooter went KAPOWWW!

His voice echoed, "NOT AGAIN" as he flew through the hole in the top of the circus tent.

Poor Scooter, he didn't mean to toot!

Scooter zoomed, and he soared a great distance, landing with a PLOP right into the ocean. But do not worry! Scooter is from Planet Zubot, where kittens can breathe underwater!

Scooter saw all kinds of water creatures big and small.

He said, "A wonder so great, what a beautiful place!"

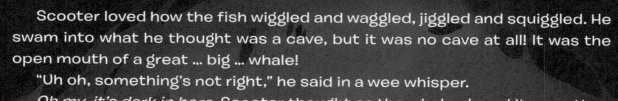

Scooter loved how the fish wiggled and waggled, jiggled and squiggled. He swam into what he thought was a cave, but it was no cave at all! It was the open mouth of a great ... big ... whale!

"Uh oh, something's not right," he said in a wee whisper.

Oh my, it's dark in here, Scooter thought as the whale closed its mouth.

Scooter's belly began to rumble and shake. Just as the whale blew water from its spout, upward and out shot Scooter as he let out a big

TOOOOOOT!

Once again, Scooter flew through the air. Can you guess where he landed next???

Scooter found himself in a great big city called Calgary, home of the horses and chuck wagons in the Great Stampede. He'd seen photos of it back home on Planet Zubot.

Scooter wandered and wondered as he came to a big concert hall. There he heard many beautiful sounds from a musical orchestra. The instruments looked very strange—not like the ones back home as he remembered them. Scooter spotted a drum and began to play along with the same strange-looking creatures he saw on the choo choo train. Just as the music began to fade to quiet, Scooter let out a big

TOOOOOOT!

All of the creatures threw their instruments into the air in a great fright.

Poor Scooter, he didn't mean to toot!

Scooter became sad as he walked the city streets. As it was getting dark outside, he saw a light from the window of a house in the distance. He went to the front door and knocked with a paw. The door opened slowly, and Scooter spoke a soft "meow."

"Aww, isn't he cute?" said the family inside. Just at that moment, Scooter went TOOOOOOT!

The parents and children went silent and looked at each other. Then they all let out a great ... big ... MUSICAL TOOOOOOT!

Scooter and the family all laughed together. Scooter felt happy and smiled from whisker to whisker. They invited him in for more fun and a long-needed cat nap.

Scooter had fun, but the fun was soon done.

"I toot all the time, and I can't seem to stop," Scooter said. "I'm a little space kitty from Planet Zubot, and I can't find my way back!"

"Have no fear, Scooter," said the Doctor Mom.

"Do not worry," said the Scientist Dad.

"A Zubiberry fell down from outer space, and I found out it lessens the great big toots!" exclaimed Doctor Mom in great joy.

Scooter popped the blue, pink, and purple swirl berry into his mouth, and as he tasted its cotton candy flavor, he remembered.

"These grow on my home planet, Zubot!"

"I found the same ingredients here on Earth that are in the Zubiberry and made them into a delicious juice," said Doctor Mom.

"Scooter, come to my workshop. I build all kinds of cars, trains, boats, airplanes, and spaceships. I will build you a spaceship your size so that you can travel back home to your family and friends!" shouted Scientist Dad with excitement.

"MOEWWWEEE, YIPEE!" Scooter bounded as he jumped in great glee!

One month later, Scooter's spaceship was complete, and he was tooting much less since he was drinking the Zubiberry juice every day.

On a bright sunny day, the family gave Scooter a farewell wish card with their last name and address on it, in case he wanted to visit them in the future, of course! Then the children gave Scooter a hug for good times. As the ship lifted up into space for the long-awaited trip home, he sipped of the juice made from Zubiberries to help stay on course.

When Scooter arrived home, he was greeted by family and friends with hugs and cheers as he shared about his adventures of wonder and hope.
   Scooter took the last gulp of the Zubiberry juice, and as he looked at the can, his whiskers went twitch. A smile formed on his happy fur face as he read ...

Love, the Zubots
Your friends from Planet Earth.
Come visit again!

About the Author

Alicia P. Zubot is an Expressive Arts Facilitator, artist, writer, and hobby musician living in Calgary, Alberta, Canada. She experienced several major surgeries throughout her childhood and early adulthood, including life-changing eye surgeries to cure congenital legal blindness. Her body functioned in ways that limited her ability to run, play, and jump at times. Like Scooter, Alicia felt shy and sometimes frustrated along her life adventure into adulthood. Yet she was lovingly embraced by family, friends, and the medical teams on her journey to adjust and recover. This empowered her to grow and discover gifts and talents. As Alicia embarked on the path to become an artist, she realized that her medical struggles were a source of courage and strength to pursue dreams beyond obstacles. In reading her story through Scooter's space journey to Earth, we can find meaning in our experiences, letting our imagination take us to new heights.

Alicia has a pet cat named Scooter, who inspired her story. And he does "toot" a lot.

Lightning Source UK Ltd.
Milton Keynes UK
UKHW052116150720
366593UK00003B/45